Ebony and
The Five Dwarfs

Ebony and The Five Dwarfs

Susan Lake

Ilustrated by Krystal 'Azzah Lake and Chynna Ellen Lake

ISBN: Softcover 978-1-4257-7841-5

This book was printed in the United States of America.

To order additional copies of this book, contact:
Xlibris Corporation
1-888-795-4274
www.Xlibris.com
Orders@Xlibris.com

38246

This book is dedicated to my brother, the late Franky Dee King:
and all the children of the world.

AUTHOR'S NOTE

"EBONY AND THE Five Dwarfs" is my own version of the classic fairy tale "Snow White and the Seven Dwarfs," by the Brothers Grimm.

This book is for all children to enjoy, especially those of color. As a young, African-American girl reading "Snow White and the Seven Dwarfs," some years ago, I believed that only the "fairest of them all" were the most beautiful in the world. I've come to realize that that was never true. Those who are the "darkest of them all" are indeed, also beautiful.

Ebony and the Five Dwarfs is a fairytale for those young children with very dark skin to cherish. Over the years, I have witnessed young black children preferring to play with white colored dolls instead of black ones. Why? – Because society continues to lead some children and adults of color to believe that their hair is "too nappy," their lips are "too big"; and their skin is "too dark." My advice to those children and adults is to ignore such ignorance and be proud of who you are – always!

Most of all, children should learn from a ripe age, to never let anyone discourage or misguide them from living up to their dreams. For those who carry hatred in their hearts, only bitterness and unhappiness will follow.

Beauty comes in many, many forms – therefore, let's love each other and accept one another for who we are.

With love,

Susan Lake

IT WAS IN a large palace in a place that would much later be known as Sierra Leone, Africa, where a queen sat at her window working. Her embroidery frame was of ebony. When she looked at the frame she said to herself, "Oh if I had a child as dark as ebony, as the color of this embroidery frame!"

Not very long after, the queen had a daughter, with skin as dark as ebony, lips as full as the moon, and tight, tight, curly brown hair. The queen died soon after giving birth.

After a year had gone by, the king took another wife, a beautiful woman, but one who was profusely proud and overbearing. The new queen stood nearly 6 feet tall, with thick brown hair that hung just above her shoulders. Her bole-colored skin was smooth, with not a mark to be found. The statuesque-looking queen could not bear to be surpassed in beauty by anyone.

For those who knew the queen, they would say amongst each other that the heiress would be far more beautiful if she smiled more.

The queen was also used to getting her way, all the time. Her servants jumped to her service because they had no other choice, if they wanted to survive. Just days into her new role as queen, she overheard one servant praising the beauty of another woman nearby. She ordered that the servant be put to death immediately. The poor man was taken atop a nearby mountain and beheaded by dusk.

The queen also had many things, in which she took advantage of nearly all of them. The queen had the most jewelry and the finest dresses of hand-woven cloth than any other local woman. But there was a special gift from the locals, that was given on the royal couple's sixteenth anniversary that the queen praised the most. That gift was a magic, 7-foot onyx statue, that stood in a corridor of the royal couple's palace. The statue represented three principles: honesty, radiance, and charm.

The queen would always stand before the shiny statue and ask, "My gracious statue in the hall, who is the darkest of us all?" The statue answered, "Queen, you are full and dark, very true, but Ebony is darker than you."

This gave the queen a great shock, because she knew the statue spoke only the truth. She hated Ebony ever since. Even though Ebony was a princess, the queen became mean towards her. The queen's anger and rage increased every day toward her stepdaughter.

When the king left the palace, the queen changed from the façade of a nice, pleasant woman to what she really was – mean and envious.

"Ebony come here!" the queen ordered.

Magical
Onyx

"Yes mother," Ebony answered as she ran into the queen's room.

"Go with the servants to find out how many bags of rutile were collected by the first group of men that I sent out. Now!" the queen demanded.

Ebony could not believe what she was hearing.

"And don't you look at me that way. Just because you are the princess, I am still the queen!"

Ebony immediately looked the other way, towards the servants and went on to do as the queen ordered.

Other orders of the queen were for servants to gather rubber, palms, diamonds and iron ore. This upset Ebony, but she did as she was told. The locals also did not think the queen treated Ebony or anyone else with respect except for her husband, the king. Through everything, Ebony never complained to the king, fearing what the queen said she would do to her if she had. The queen also threatened her servants. She made it known to the servants that if they were to breathe a word about what was going on between her and Ebony, she would order, "Off with their head!"

Although the work that Ebony was ordered to do was tough, she had grown used to it as time went by. She waxed the marble floors and shined every column in the palace, from top to bottom. Without the queen knowing, Ebony even offered to help the other servants with their duties but they declined, for they all felt sorry for the beautiful princess.

But one day, Ebony grew tired of the queen's ways and refused one order to bring her wood.

"Mother, I am very tired and worn," the princess said. "I cannot do anymore."

"What did you say?" the queen asked while walking toward Ebony, but at that very moment the king walked through the door.

The queen quickly turned to her husband and greeted him with a smile, showing her beautiful pearly white teeth. Although mean, the queen's beauty was indeed striking and the king fell weak to her.

"My love, how are you today?" the king asked his wife before kissing her cheek.

"Ebony and I were just telling the servants what we think you would like for dinner tonight," the queen said with another fake smile.

"My darling Ebony, why is your fine dress full of dirt?" the king asked with a look of wonder.

"Father, I slipped while walking through the garden," Ebony replied, looking at the queen's expression.

The queen continued to stand tall, then bowed her head to grin.

"Ebony, darling. You are always into something," the queen said as she walked out of the room. "I'll get someone to clean you up right now my dear."

After dinner was served and everyone went to bed, the queen went over to her onyx statue. The king always said nice things to his wife, which made her even more proud. So she stood before her favorite gift and asked, "My gracious statue in the hall, who is the darkest of us all?" The statue answered, "Queen, you are full and dark, very true, but Ebony is darker than you."

The queen could not sleep well after hearing the honest words of the statue. By morning the queen sent for a huntsman and said, "Take Ebony out into the rainforest and put her to death. Bring me her heart for a token." The huntsman consented and then led Ebony away to the rainforest, which was miles away.

But when the huntsman drew his spear he couldn't after hearing Ebony beg for mercy. She promised to go even further out into the rainforest and never come home again.

On the way home, the huntsman killed a young wild boar, took out its heart and brought it to the queen. The heart was seasoned and cooked and the wicked woman ate it up, thinking that Ebony lived no more.

Meanwhile, Ebony was scared for her life out in the rainforest, fearing the wild animals. But the animals did Ebony no harm, for she was far too beautiful. Ebony ran anyway and when the evening drew near, she came to a small bamboo hut next to a large tree where a spider monkey hung. The spider monkey motioned to Ebony with one of its long arms pointed toward the hut, as if telling the princess not to fear what's inside. Ebony knocked on the door, but there was no answer. The tired princess then went inside to rest.

Everything in the hut was very small, but immaculate. In one corner, there were five small wooden bowls and spoons atop a low, squared table. Ebony, having been very hungry and thirsty, ate from each bowl a little rice and fish and drank out of each cup a drop of wine.

Ebony soon fell asleep on one of five tiny beds rowed alongside a wall, opposite the table she had stood minutes before.

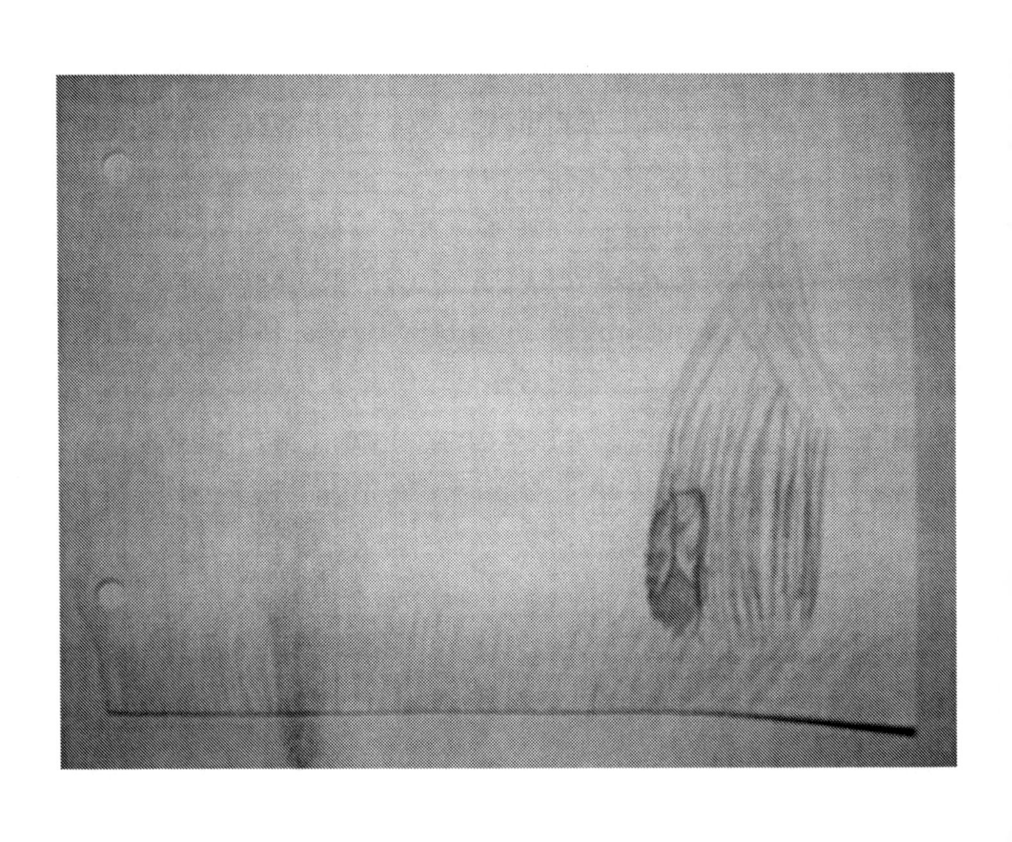

Into the night the masters of the hut came home. They were five male dwarfs, whose occupation was to educate children in a nearby village. The dwarfs' names were Cheerful, Brilliant, Moody, Kooky and Timid.

"Oh what a wonderful day it was," Cheerful said as he walked through the door.

The dwarfs immediately noticed that someone must have been in their home, as everything was not in the same order in which they had left it.

"Look! Oh my," Cheery said, pointing to Ebony who was still sound asleep on his bed.

Each dwarf smiled, even Moody, for they had admired Ebony's beauty so. They did not wake her, but just stared and after a while went about their normal routine of bathing, eating, reading, then going to bed. Cheery slept on the floor, cuddled in a blanket.

"Let us make it as comfy as can be for the beautiful one," Brilliant advised the others, who each replied with a nod.

By morning, Ebony awoke and saw the five dwarfs just staring at her. She was very frightened, but most of the dwarfs seemed quite friendly as they introduced themselves. Ebony then told the five little men how she had wound up in their home.

"Well you can't just come walking into people's homes my dear," Moody said upsettingly.

"Hey, what did I say? We want to make things as comfy as possible for the beautiful one," Brilliant said, glaring at Moody.

Then Brilliant turned to Ebony, "If you will keep our house for us, and cook, and wash, and make the beds, and keep everything clean, you may stay with us, and you shall lack nothing."

Ebony was all smiles.

"Yes! Certainly," she replied.

Kooky then let out a goofy-sounding laugh, while Timid had not said one word through everything.

Ebony performed her duties, as days went by. She answered the door to nobody – just as the dwarfs had ordered.

Now the queen, having eaten Ebony's heart, so she thought, felt quite sure that now she was the first and darkest, and so she came to her statue to ask, "My gracious statue in the hall, who is the darkest of us all?"

The statue answered, "Queen, your great beauty is rare, but Ebony living in a hut – two miles into the rainforest – with five dwarfs is a thousand times darker."

The statue's reply made the queen very angry, for the queen knew that the huntsman must have deceived her. The queen thought and thought about how she could manage to destroy Ebony. Finally, she came up with a plan.

The queen disguised herself as an old, poor woman. She then proceeded through the rainforest, dodging wild animals. She finally reached the five dwarfs' hut. A large toucan then gave a call, warning the other animals that a very troublesome creature had entered their rainforest.

"Quiet you bird!" the queen snapped.

The old, poor woman turned from the toucan, ignoring its continuous cry, and knocked on the door. Ebony looked through the peephole and thought, "I need not be afraid of letting in this old woman." So she opened the door.

The old woman held out her hand and begged for some food. When Ebony turned her back, on her way to the fruit bowl, the old woman drew a piece of rope she had had around her waist. The old woman then swiftly looped the rope around Ebony's long neck, then pulled and pulled until Ebony collapsed to the floor.

"Now I am the darkest of them all," said the old woman as she ran away, with the animals chasing behind.

Not long after the old woman fled the hut, the dwarfs returned home. They were terrified to see their dear Ebony lying on the floor, motionless. Brilliant turned Ebony onto her back and resuscitated her with his special touch.

When the dwarfs heard what had happened, they'd figured that the old woman was none other than the wicked queen. The queen had a bad reputation, even on their end of town, because she was very envious. The dwarfs actually scolded Ebony for having let someone in when they weren't home.

When the queen got home she went straight to the onyx statue and asked, "My gracious statue in the hall, who is the darkest of us all?"

The statue answered, "Queen, your beauty is rare, but Ebony living in a hut – two miles into the rainforest – with five dwarfs is a thousand times darker."

This shocked the queen so, for she knew that Ebony must still be alive.

The wicked queen came up with another scheme in an attempt to rid of Ebony. By witchcraft she made a poisoned comb. Then the queen disguised herself, to look like a different old woman. The queen was fully aware that she needed to enter the rainforest quietly because the animals had sensed her wickedness.

While entering the rainforest for a second time, the queen wore closed shoes to hide her feet. A mass of giant ants bit at the queen's feet during her first attempt to rid of Ebony, when she had worn sandals. The queen again made it to the five dwarfs' hut and knocked on the door, while ignoring the cries of that same toucan. The queen's line this time was, "Good wares to sell! Good wares to sell!"

A more cautious Ebony said, "Go away, I can not let anybody in."

"But you are not forbidden to look," the jealous woman said. "Now for once your tight, tight hair shall be properly combed."

Poor Ebony, thinking no harm, let the old woman do as she would, but sooner was the comb put in her hair than the poison began to work after making contact with her scalp. Ebony's vision blurred and then the poor girl fell down senseless. The old woman smiled and then fled, with even more animals chasing her than the first time. The luck of the queen was plentiful, as she just missed being taken by a boa.

"Ha! Not quite my friend," the queen said in a cynical tone while the snake slithered in the opposite direction.

A short while later, the five dwarfs came home. They saw Ebony lying on the ground, and knew that it was the queen's doing. The men found the poisoned comb, and no sooner had they drawn it out of her hair than Ebony came to herself and related all that had passed.

All five dwarfs scolded Ebony for opening the door to someone when they weren't home.

By then, the queen was home before her onyx statue.

"My gracious statue in the hall, who is the darkest of us all?"

The statue answered, "Queen, your great beauty is rare, but Ebony living in a hut – two miles into the rainforest – with five dwarfs is a thousand times darker."

Upon hearing the statue's reply, the queen trembled and shook with anger.

"Ebony shall dic. She shall die I say!" the queen cried.

The queen made a poisonous bowl of wild berries, disguised herself as a peasant woman and headed toward the five dwarfs' home.

When the queen knocked on the door saying, "Berries for sale! Berries for sale," Ebony declined to answer.

"Come, come now sweetie. These delicious berries are irresistible," the peasant woman said.

The berries were perfect looking. So perfect looking that Ebony could not resist opening the door to taste them.

No more than two seconds had passed before Ebony fell to the floor, dead.

Behind that, the queen let out a laugh so loud the lions roared.

"This time none of the five dwarfs will be able to bring you to life again sweetie!" the queen laughed.

When the queen went before the statue, it had finally given her the answer she had longed for.

"You are the darkest now, of all," the statue said.

It was then that the queen's envious heart had peace.

The five dwarfs came home that evening only to find Ebony's lifeless body on the floor. They laid her on Cheery's bed, washed her up with water and wine, combed her hair, but all was of no avail. Poor Ebony was dead. The five dwarfs wept for three whole days.

"We cannot hide her away in the black ground," Timid said.

The dwarfs made a coffin of clear glass, so as to be looked into from all sides, and they laid Ebony in it. The dwarfs then wrote in golden letters upon it Ebony's name and that she was a king's daughter. Then the five dwarfs placed the coffin out upon a nearby hill.

No animals bothered the coffin for the young woman inside was just too beautiful. In fact, they had all mourned.

Days went by, but Ebony's fine appearance never changed – for she looked as if she were asleep.

It happened, however, that one day a king's son, from a nearby village, rode through the rainforest on a horse. He saw on the hill the coffin and beautiful Ebony inside of it. The king's son then read what was written in golden letters upon the coffin.

"Let me have the coffin and I will give you whatever you like to ask for it," he said to the dwarfs.

But the dwarfs told him that they could not part with the coffin for all the riches in the world. But the king's son said, "I beseech you to give it to me, for I cannot live without looking at this beautiful creature. If you consent, I will bring you great honor. I will then care for you as if you were my brethren."

By this time, the dwarfs felt sorry for the king's son and gave him the coffin. He called the servants and bid them to carry the coffin away on their shoulders.

Now it happened as the king's son was going along his merry way with the coffin, he stumbled over a bush. The impact caused bits of poisoned berries to fly out of Ebony's throat. It was not long before Ebony opened her eyes, threw up the cover of the coffin and sat up alive and well.

"Where am I?" Ebony cried.

The king's son answered, "You are near me," after relating all that had happened. "I would rather have you than anything in the world; come with me to my father's palace and you shall be my bride.

Ebony followed the handsome man to the palace where they married. The wedding was a ceremony of tribal dance, music and feast.

Ebony's stepmother had also been invited to the feast. When the queen had dressed herself in beautiful clothes, she went to her statue and asked, "My gracious statue in the hall, who is the darkest of us all?"

The statue answered, "Oh queen, your great beauty is rare, but the young bride is a thousand times more darker."

The queen threw a temper tantrum in the hallway, by screaming and stomping her feet wildly. First, the queen thought she would not go to the wedding. But, then the queen felt that no peace would come upon her until she went and saw the bride. When the queen saw Ebony, she felt as if her heart had sunk to the ground.

The queen's hatred for Ebony was so great that it became unhealthy. The queen suffered ulcers and her beautiful looks began to fade from stress. The king also became angry at his wife, after a servant could not bear to hold in what the queen was doing to his daughter. The king promised the servant's safety and this made the queen very, very bitter. The queen felt helpless after losing respect from her husband and everyone else in town. Also, every time the queen heard Ebony's name, her bitterness increased.

The next day, the queen saw Ebony and her new husband embracing through a palace window. That site was way too much for the envious queen to handle. Within moments, she had fallen to her death from a heart attack before the palace's front door.

As the years went by, Ebony and her loving prince remained close at heart. As for the five dwarfs, their trust that nothing could ever end the couple's union remained strong.

The five dwarfs mainly knew that nothing, particularly the evil, could ever stop Ebony from living the life that she was destined to have.

THE END

Printed in the United States
154602LV00003B/44/A

9 781425 778415